THE
PHONE BOOK

INSTANT COMMUNICATION FROM SMOKE SIGNALS TO SATELLITES AND BEYOND...

Written by
Elizabeth MacLeod

Illustrated by
Bill Slavin

Kids Can Press Ltd.
Toronto

With all my love to Paul — thanks for giving me a r-r-r-i-n-g!

ACKNOWLEDGEMENTS

Very special thanks to Paul Wilson, technical consultant, who explained concepts in telecommunications and carefully checked both the text and illustrations. Many thanks also to the following people who gave generously of their time and knowledge: the staff at Bell Canada's Historical Collection; Robert Devries, Cantel; Suneet S. Tuli, WideCom Group Inc.; librarians at the Metropolitan Toronto Reference Library. Thanks also to the many people on the Internet who helped answer my questions about telecommunications.

It was a real pleasure working with the book's illustrator, Bill Slavin, and designer, Esperança Melo. I really appreciate the concern, care and fun Bill brought to the illustrations and the creativity and clarity of Esperança's design.

Many thanks to the staff at Kids Can Press for their help and support, especially Lori Burwash, Ricky Englander and Valerie Hussey. Special thanks to my editor, Val Wyatt, who brought so much fun and life to this book and to the whole process of writing it. Thank you, Val, for your patience and care.

Technical consultant: Paul Wilson

Kids Can Press Ltd. acknowledges with appreciation the assistance of the Canada Council and the Ontario Arts Council in the production of this book.

Canadian Cataloguing in Publication Data

MacLeod, Elizabeth
     The phone book : instant communication from smoke signals to satellites and beyond —

Includes index.
ISBN 1-55074-220-5

1. Telecommunication — Juvenile literature.
2. Telephone — Juvenile literature. 3. Communication — Juvenile literature. I. Slavin, Bill. II. Title.

TK5102.4.M33   1995   j621.382   C94-932584-8

Kids Can Press Ltd.
29 Birch Avenue
Toronto, Ontario, Canada
M4V 1E2

Edited by Valerie Wyatt
Designed by Esperança Melo
Printed and bound in Hong Kong

95 0 9 8 7 6 5 4 3 2 1

CONTENTS

ON THE PHONE

Rats!! You've forgotten your math assignment. You pick up the phone and dial your friend Kate. She's not home, so you leave an SOS on her family's answering machine. Then you phone Tim. Bingo! He faxes you the assignment. The telephone (and its cousin the facsimile machine) have saved your life.

Telephones not only make it easier to find out about homework, they also connect you with friends and relatives, get help fast in an emergency and let you buy concert tickets, pizzas and even clothes, without ever leaving home. Phone relatives such as fax machines, cellular phones and modems make communication even more convenient.

How was the telephone invented? How can we talk to people on the other side of the world? How can a fax machine send stuff instantly from one place to another? To find out the answers to these questions and a lot more, turn the page. But first ... maybe you should finish your math homework.

Before telephones

Suppose you were a cave person living thousands of years ago. As you're lounging in your cave entrance one day, you spot a herd of woolly mammoths thundering towards you. Yikes! You have to warn your cousin Gronk, who lives 20 caves over. But how? You could send your brother Blog running over with the message. (Nobody can write yet, so Blog better have a good memory.) Blog's busy? Get out the drums or send a smoke signal. Definitely low tech.

If you lived a little later, say about 3500 B.C., when people knew how to write, you wouldn't have to depend on Blog's memory, so you could send a longer message. You wouldn't have to depend on his feet either: you could send the message by horse, sailing ship or homing pigeon. If you lived in Persia, your message could be shouted from one tower to the next by men with powerful voices — and good lungs!

Too slow? The Greeks thought so too, so around 500 B.C. they developed the visual telegraph. They built a series of brick walls just close enough together to see from one wall to the next. Indentations along the top of the wall represented each letter of the alphabet. To send your message, you lit fires in the correct indents. Someone on the next wall would see the fires and relay your message.

Later, books and daily news sheets made exchanging information easier. However, even as late as the eighteenth century, news still moved no faster than people on horseback or shipboard. Mail service made sending messages easier and cheaper, but not faster.

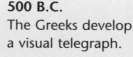

20 000 B.C.
Prehistoric people passed along news from person to person.

3500 B.C.
First written language

500 B.C.
The Greeks develop a visual telegraph.

1793
Claude Chappé invents a signalling system.

It wasn't until the late 1700s that French engineer Claude Chappé really sped up long-distance communication. He created a "telegraph" similar to the one back in Greece. Towers were built between Paris and other major cities in France, each topped by a huge crossbar with two arms. An operator moved the crossbar and arms to spell out a message, which was read through a telescope by the operator in the next tower. Messages were passed along from tower to tower at the lightning speed of 120 km (75 miles) per minute. By the mid-1800s most of Europe used Chappé's system.

Around 1816 you could communicate using flags of various colours and patterns in different positions. This system could transmit 8000 symbols. Not only were there too many to remember, but the code book was constantly being changed. Despite its problems, this system was useful for ships trying to talk to nearby ships.

On land, steam-powered trains transported messages around the world faster than horses could manage. Still not fast enough? By the mid-1700s scientists were working on transmitting electric signals. These were instant — but experts didn't have a way to control them and use them to transmit information. Then along came Samuel F.B. Morse with an electric telegraph system that worked. Finally you could warn Gronk instantly of danger. Only one problem — woolly mammoths had been extinct for centuries.

1816
Ships use flag-signalling systems.

1844
Morse invents the telegraph.

1866
A telegraph cable links Europe and North America.

1876
Alexander Graham Bell invents the telephone.

Samuel Morse's telegraph

The key to Samuel Morse's electric telegraph was the electromagnet. You still depend on it when you listen to the radio, watch television, ring a doorbell, ride in a car — and talk on the telephone.

What is an electromagnet? It is made of a battery and a piece of metal wrapped with thin wire. It's easy to make one — try it yourself using the instructions on page 9. How does it work? When electricity flows through the wire, a tiny magnetic field is created. If the wire is wrapped around a piece of metal, the metal becomes magnetic, too. Because the magnet depends on electricity for its power, it's called an electromagnet.

The electromagnet was important to inventors because it allowed them to control magnetism and turn it on and off as they wished.

The first electromagnet was built around 1825. Samuel Morse used it to develop the telegraph, which you see here.

TOO LATE!

Just how important is instant communication? The War of 1812 would probably never have happened if the telegraph had been invented by then.

The war began because Great Britain was interfering with US ships. So, on June 18, 1812, the United States declared war. But two days before, Britain had promised to stop meddling. Too late — the fighting began before the message was received in North America.

Make an electromagnet

You'll need:

- about 3 m (10 feet) of thin, plastic-covered wire
- a large iron or steel nail or bolt, about 8 cm (3 inches) long
- a sharp knife (get permission from an adult before you use it)
- masking tape
- a C or D battery (the same type you use in a flashlight)
- paper-clips, pins or other small metal objects

1. Wrap the wire neatly around the nail or bolt so that the loops are right beside each other. The more loops, the stronger your magnet will be. Make sure you leave about 15 cm (6 inches) of the wire sticking out at each end.

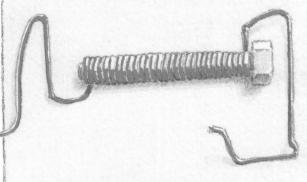

2. Using the knife, scrape about 2 cm (1 inch) of the plastic covering off the ends of the wire.

3. With the masking tape, attach one end of the wire to one end of the battery. (It doesn't matter which end.) Be sure to tape it securely.

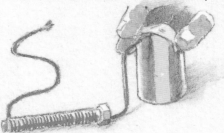

4. Press the other end of the wire to the other end of the battery and hold your magnet near paper-clips or pins. What happens? Remove the wire from the end of the battery and see what the paper-clips do.

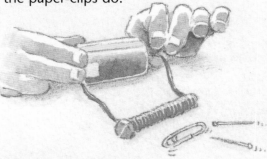

What happens?

You've turned the coiled wire and nail into an electromagnet. Touch the end of the wire to the battery and you complete an electric circuit that supplies electricity to the wire. As the wire conducts the electric current, a small magnetic field forms around the wire, turning it and the nail it's wrapped around into a magnet.

You can use your magnet to pick up paper-clips, pins and other metal objects. When you remove one of the ends of the wire from the battery, you interrupt the circuit. The magnetic field stops and the paper-clips drop.

- How can you make your magnet stronger? Does changing the size of the nail help? What if you add another layer of loops?

- How else could you use a magnet that you can turn on and off?

9

Dot-dash-dot Dot Dot-dash Dash-dot-dot
Dash Dot-dot-dot-dot Dot-dot Dot-dot-dot

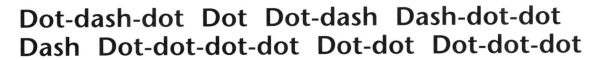

The electromagnet made it possible to create an electric current and to turn it on and off at will. That gave Samuel Morse an idea. Why not make up a code of "ons" and "offs" so that people could send messages over a wire? Morse thought of a short interruption in the current as a "dot." A longer one he called a "dash." He combined the dots and dashes to make a code for every letter in the alphabet, as you can see on the next page. An operator would send a message in Morse code and another operator at the other end of the wire would write down the dots and dashes, then decode them and get the message.

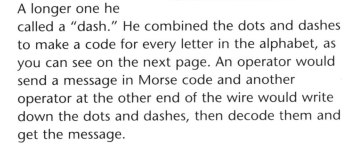

Morse called his invention the telegraph. "Tele" comes from the Greek for "far off" and "graph" means an instrument that records something — in this case, electric impulses. He spent 12 years working on his invention. There were many problems to solve before it could connect distant cities. The biggest challenge was that the electric current wasn't strong enough to carry messages through long stretches of wire. So Morse invented an electric relay that boosted the current along the way.

The first telegraph message was sent on May 24, 1844, from Washington, DC, to Baltimore, Maryland, a distance of 60 km (37 miles). The message Morse sent was "What hath God wrought?" These words expressed how amazing the telegraph was. By the 1860s most cities were linked by telegraph lines and information was finally moving at the speed of electricity. Telegraph cables were laid beneath the Atlantic Ocean to link Europe and North America. For the first time, news from around the world could be read in newspapers the same day it happened.

— · — Send it in Morse code — · · —

This is International Morse Code, a simplified version of Morse's original code.

A · —	N — ·	1 · — — — —	6 — · · · ·
B — · · ·	O — — —	2 · · — — —	7 — — · · ·
C — · — ·	P · — — ·	3 · · · — —	8 — — — · ·
D — · ·	Q — — · —	4 · · · · —	9 — — — — ·
E ·	R · — ·	5 · · · · ·	0 — — — — —
F · · — ·	S · · ·		
G — — ·	T —		
H · · · ·	U · · —	Period · — · — · —	
I · ·	V · · · —	Comma — — · · — —	
J · — — —	W · — —	SOS · · · — — — · · ·	
K — · —	X — · · —	Start — · —	
L · — · ·	Y — · — —	End of message · — · — ·	
M — —	Z — — · ·	Error · · · · · · · ·	

- Using your index finger or the end of a pencil, try sending a message in Morse code. Tap your finger for the "dots" and scratch lightly for the "dashes." (Do this on a surface you can't damage!) How fast are you?
- Try tapping out SOS, the international signal for distress. The letters don't stand for anything, but they are easy to remember and transmit.
- Have your friend tap a Morse code message for you to decode. Does her tapping sound different from yours? People who send lots of Morse messages develop a certain rhythm. Experienced coders can recognize another person's rhythm or "fist." Today that's more difficult because some senders or "hams" use computers to generate their dots and dashes.
- Can you develop a new code to send secret messages?

I KNOW MORSE CODE.

I KNOT HORSE TOES??

THE MAN BEHIND THE CODE

Samuel Morse was a well-known artist before he was a scientist. He painted portraits of famous businessmen and politicians, including American president James Monroe. But in 1832, while he was sailing home to the United States after a trip to Europe, he met a scientist who was studying the electromagnet. Morse became fascinated with the electromagnet, and life has never been the same since.

Inventing the telephone

Alexander Graham Bell

It was one thing to send simple dots and dashes over the wires. But what about something more complicated — like music or the human voice? In Boston, Massachusetts, a young teacher of the deaf heard about Morse's telegraph and decided to experiment with sending sound over wires. The young man's name was Alexander Graham Bell (or AGB, for short).

You might say that AGB inherited his interest in sound from his father, a professor of speech in Edinburgh, Scotland. Professor Bell had invented a code called "visible speech," a way of describing the position and action of the throat, tongue and lips for making various sounds. He and his sons often gave demonstrations of the system.

To encourage the boys' interest in sound, Professor Bell took them to see a mechanical doll that could "speak." AGB and his brother built a copy of the doll's head and got it to say, "Mama." The voice must have sounded quite real: the brothers had to end their experiments when neighbours complained about a baby's crying.

AGB was so interested in the mechanical doll he had seen that he kept experimenting with sound and how to reproduce and transmit it. A friend lent him a book about sound experiments and AGB was fascinated by it. Because the book was in German, he misunderstood what it said and began to think of transmitting speech over wires — the idea the telephone is based on.

AGB experimented with all sorts of sounds. When he was 20, he tried an experiment on the family dog. By massaging the vocal cords of his terrier, he hoped to make it "speak." Once he actually got it to growl out "Ow-ah-oo, ga-ma-ma." Say it fast and it sounds like "How are you, Grandmama."

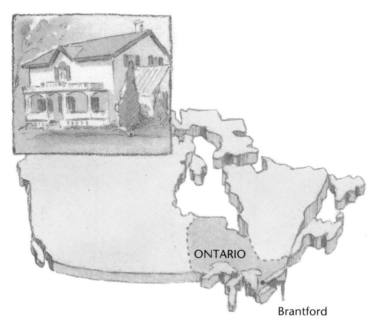

ONTARIO

Brantford

When his father began teaching visible speech at a school for the deaf in Boston, AGB followed him. He too began to work with deaf children, teaching them to speak. While he taught, AGB continued to experiment with sending sounds over a wire. He started with music.

In 1870, when AGB was 23 years old, his family moved to Brantford, Ontario, where he worked on various sound experiments. One project was to transcribe the language of the Six Nations people who lived on a nearby reserve into visible speech. For his work, he was made an honorary chief.

In 1860 a German inventor named Philipp Reis had created a device that used a sausage skin to transmit musical tones over a wire. The sound was poor. AGB thought he had a better idea. To help him, he hired an engineer named Thomas A. Watson.

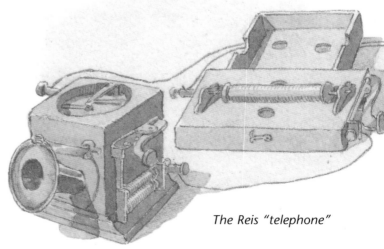

The Reis "telephone"

AGB's idea was to use several pairs of identical tuning forks to send different tones over a wire at the same time and then separate out tones at the other end. He placed twin A of the pair at one end of a wire, and twin B at the opposite end. When he struck twin A, it would send vibrations over the wire.

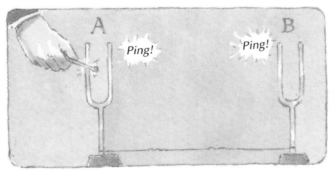

Twin B would pick up the vibrations from its twin, vibrate and make the same sound. This process is called "sympathetic vibrations." Try "Sound a note" on the next page to see how it works.

The two men spent months working on AGB's idea, but the tuning forks didn't transmit sound as AGB had hoped. The problem was that the twins didn't always recognize each other. They picked up vibrations from other tuning forks and the sounds got jumbled together.

So AGB decided to try steel reeds instead of tuning forks. Some musical instruments, such as oboes, have reeds. When someone blows into the mouthpiece of an oboe, the reed vibrates and your ear hears the vibrations as musical notes. With reeds, and a lot of experimenting, AGB was finally able to complete what he called the harmonic telegraph. It could send up to 40 Morse code messages at the same time. The telegraph companies loved the idea.

Then AGB began working on a new device. He hoped that, by using lots of reeds, he could transmit lots of sounds, even the complex variety of sounds in the human voice. AGB called his invention a harp transmitter. He didn't have the equipment or skill to make it, so it was never more than a sketch. But thinking about it took him one step closer to transmitting the sounds of the human voice and so send conversations over wires.

AGB never built the harp transmitter but he created a detailed sketch of it.

Sound a note

AGB knew that sound vibrations from one object can make another object vibrate the same way. By using these sympathetic vibrations, he hoped to transmit sounds. Start up some sympathetic vibrations of your own and see what happens.

You'll need:
- two identical glass pop bottles
- a friend

1. Place one bottle on a table and have your friend hold her ear close to it as shown.

2. Stand the other bottle about 30 cm (1 foot) away and blow across the top of it until you produce a clear note. Can your friend hear the sound coming from *her* bottle?

What happens?

When you blow across the bottle, you start the air vibrating. Those vibrations start the other bottle vibrating. Because the second bottle is identical to the first, it responds to vibrations the same way — it produces the same sound.

- Ask a friend to hold down the rightmost foot pedal on a piano, then open the piano and sing into it. Can you hear sympathetic vibrations?

At the other end of the line

Transmitting sound was only half the problem in inventing the telephone. The other half was *receiving* the sound.

AGB knew he needed a way to turn the electric current coming over a wire into sound. But how? One day he looked closely at a phonoautograph he was using to help deaf children learn to speak out loud. It had a stretched piece of rubber-like material called a membrane that vibrated when sound was made near it. The vibrating membrane caused a brush attached to it to trace rough patterns on smoked glass, so the children could *see* how loudly or softly they were speaking.

AGB was struck by an idea: the phonoautograph was like an eardrum. When sound reaches your ear it makes your eardrum vibrate. Tiny bones in your ear pick up the movements and pass them down through a tube of liquid to your nerves. These "auditory nerves" send the sound along to your brain, and you hear.

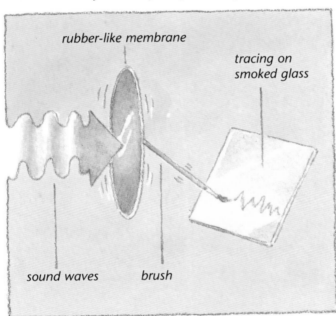

rubber-like membrane

tracing on smoked glass

sound waves   brush

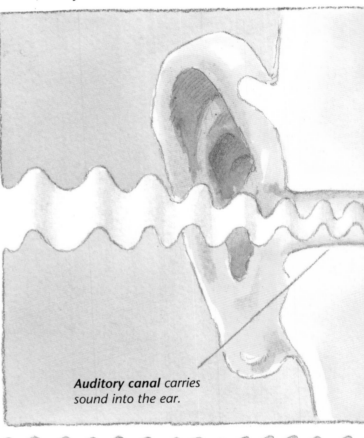

Auditory canal carries sound into the ear.

WHAT'S A TELEPHONE?

a) A cone-shaped device you can use to project your voice?

c) An invention used to order pizza?

b) A "speaking tube," once built into houses and ships so people on different floors could communicate?

AGB decided to try to make a receiver that was similar to a human ear. He mentioned his idea to a doctor friend, and a few days later an ear arrived in the mail! It had come from a corpse at a medical school.

What amazed AGB about the ear was that a very thin eardrum could make the much heavier bones of the ear vibrate. He thought of using a thin iron disc instead of a membrane and an even heavier metal lever to replace the bones.

Now that he had a receiver that would *receive* sound, AGB went back to working on a way to *transmit* sound. Since sound travels in waves, he needed a wavy electric current. In his harp transmitter, he had tried using vibrating reeds to make an electromagnet produce a varying current. This time he decided to borrow an idea from the receiver. The telephone was almost here.

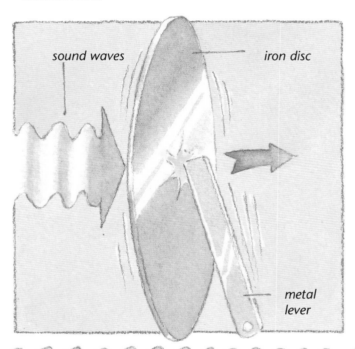

Small bones called **ossicles** transmit the vibrations to the cochlea.

Eardrum changes sounds into vibrations.

Cochlea sends signals to the brain.

sound waves

iron disc

metal lever

The answer is "all of the above." Around 1780 what we now call a megaphone (answer a) was known as a telephone. Later on, so were speaking tubes (answer b).

AGB wasn't the only person who invented what we know as the telephone. Between 1860 and 1900 many electric telephones were invented. But the best one was made by AGB. It set the pattern for the telephones we use today.

The telephone looked like this in 1876. This version was known as a liquid transmitter.

"Mr. Watson, come here. I want you."

AGB and Watson worked hard on his latest idea. Finally, on June 2, 1875, they had a breakthrough. AGB was in one room and Watson was in another. Each had a similar device: a set of thin strips of steel mounted above an electromagnet. A wire connected the two devices.

AGB was working on his device, trying to create enough current to transmit sound. In the other room, Watson noticed that one of the metal strips on his device seemed to be stuck, so he plucked it loose. AGB heard a loud twang over the wire! He rushed in to Watson to see what had happened. Watson's metal strip had vibrated, causing the electromagnet to produce a current of electricity. This current varied in intensity — it was wavy. The wavy current travelled to AGB's device, where he heard the twang.

They repeated the experiment over and over again. Every time Watson plucked the metal strip, AGB could hear it. But could the strip be made to move by using the voice instead of a finger? If so, the telephone could transmit speech.

AGB continued to work on his telephone. He designed a mechanism to receive the vibrations that would force the reed inside it to respond to the vibrations of the voice. When AGB spoke into it, Watson could hear faint whispers at the other end of the line. But neither man was satisfied — the sound wasn't clear enough.

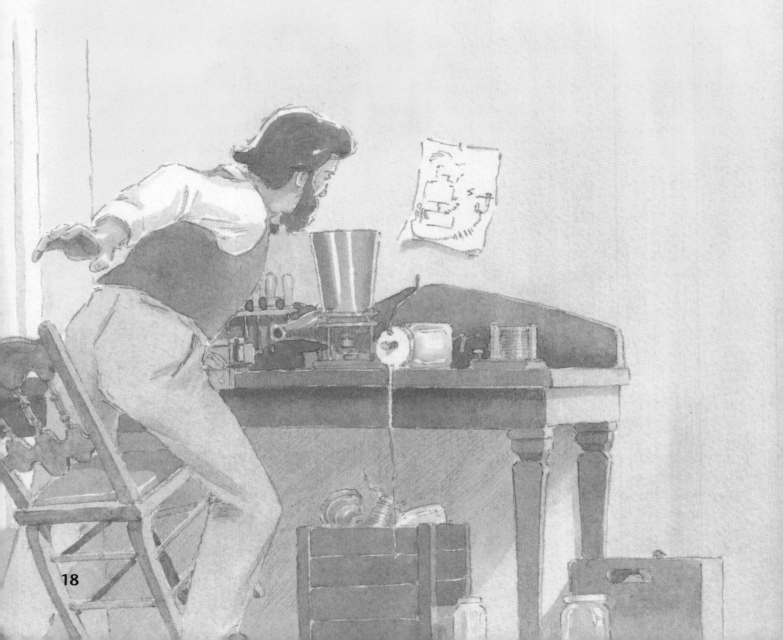

AGB and Watson were exhausted but they knew they were close to success, so they kept on working. One night a tired AGB accidentally spilled battery acid on himself. It burned through his pants and he yelled, "Mr. Watson, come here. I want you."

Watson came running. He had heard AGB all right. But he'd been too far away to hear his yell. He'd heard AGB over the telephone! "Mr. Bell," he gasped, "I distinctly heard every word you said." It was March 10, 1876. The acid spill was forgotten as they celebrated their long years of work. Finally, they had a telephone that clearly transmitted human voices.

HOY! HOY!

Hallooooo...

If AGB had had his way, we wouldn't say "Hello" when we pick up the phone, but "Hoy! Hoy!" That's how he always answered.

Not everyone says "Hello" when they answer the phone. Many British people say "Are you there?" Germans tend to give their last name. Some Americans say "Howdy!" Other people just say "Yes?" How do you answer the phone? Chances are you say the same thing as your parents or friends. Make a phone survey and find out.

The first not-so-long-distance call

AGB wanted to find out how his telephone worked over long distances. He went to his parents' home in Brantford and strung wires from the house to the garden. The phone worked — but it wasn't a very long distance.

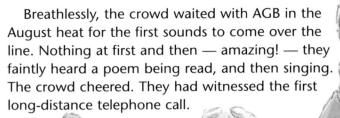

Breathlessly, the crowd waited with AGB in the August heat for the first sounds to come over the line. Nothing at first and then — amazing! — they faintly heard a poem being read, and then singing. The crowd cheered. They had witnessed the first long-distance telephone call.

The next test for the telephone was to be between the Bell home and Mount Pleasant, a town about 3 km (2 miles) away. Instead of stringing a phone line all that way, AGB decided to use the telegraph line. In order to connect the Bell home to the telegraph line, he bought up all the stove wire in town. Then he called on his neighbours to help him string it. One boy even crawled through a culvert with it.

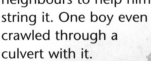

AGB didn't stop there. He planned to make a call between Brantford and Paris, Ontario. The distance was an astonishing 10 km (6 miles). Could it be done? AGB asked the Dominion Telegraph Company for permission to use their line. "Ridiculous," thought the general manager, and he threw away AGB's letter. Luckily, the manager's assistant was able to convince his boss to let AGB go ahead.

AGB and Watson were exhausted but they knew they were close to success, so they kept on working. One night a tired AGB accidentally spilled battery acid on himself. It burned through his pants and he yelled, "Mr. Watson, come here. I want you."

Watson came running. He had heard AGB all right. But he'd been too far away to hear his yell. He'd heard AGB over the telephone! "Mr. Bell," he gasped, "I distinctly heard every word you said." It was March 10, 1876. The acid spill was forgotten as they celebrated their long years of work. Finally, they had a telephone that clearly transmitted human voices.

HOY! HOY!

Hallooooo...

If AGB had had his way, we wouldn't say "Hello" when we pick up the phone, but "Hoy! Hoy!" That's how he always answered.

Not everyone says "Hello" when they answer the phone. Many British people say "Are you there?" Germans tend to give their last name. Some Americans say "Howdy!" Other people just say "Yes?" How do you answer the phone? Chances are you say the same thing as your parents or friends. Make a phone survey and find out.

The first not-so-long-distance call

AGB wanted to find out how his telephone worked over long distances. He went to his parents' home in Brantford and strung wires from the house to the garden. The phone worked — but it wasn't a very long distance.

The next test for the telephone was to be between the Bell home and Mount Pleasant, a town about 3 km (2 miles) away. Instead of stringing a phone line all that way, AGB decided to use the telegraph line. In order to connect the Bell home to the telegraph line, he bought up all the stove wire in town. Then he called on his neighbours to help him string it. One boy even crawled through a culvert with it.

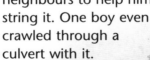

Breathlessly, the crowd waited with AGB in the August heat for the first sounds to come over the line. Nothing at first and then — amazing! — they faintly heard a poem being read, and then singing. The crowd cheered. They had witnessed the first long-distance telephone call.

AGB didn't stop there. He planned to make a call between Brantford and Paris, Ontario. The distance was an astonishing 10 km (6 miles). Could it be done? AGB asked the Dominion Telegraph Company for permission to use their line. "Ridiculous," thought the general manager, and he threw away AGB's letter. Luckily, the manager's assistant was able to convince his boss to let AGB go ahead.

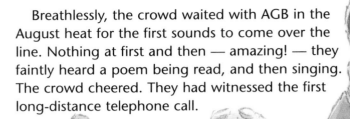

On August 10, 1876, AGB drove to Paris with his telephone and set it up at the shoe store that housed the telegraph office. At first his only companion was the telegraph operator, but soon there were so many people that the shop door had to be bolted shut. Nervously, AGB sat down at his telephone. It was time for the test.

A sound came over the wire, but faintly. The crowd murmured in disappointment. This early telephone worked only one way — AGB could receive but not send — so he telegraphed instructions to Brantford to adjust the line. Soon the voices were clear!

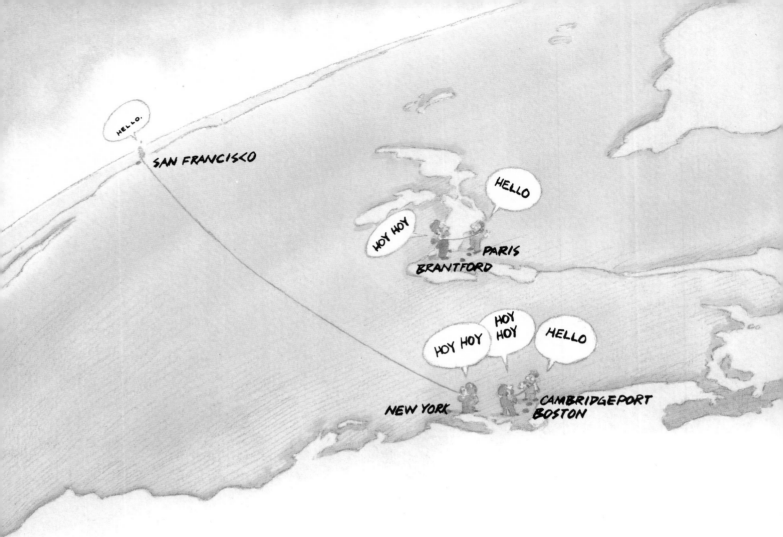

Then a familiar voice came over the line. AGB was dumbfounded. It sounded like his father, but AGB knew Professor Bell was away. Maybe the telephone distorted voices so badly that it would never be of any use. Anxiously he telegraphed to ask whose voice he had heard. A voice boomed down the line, "Yes, my son, this is your father speaking." At the last minute Dr. Bell had realized he couldn't miss his son's big moment. The telephone was a success.

There were more long-distance firsts to come. A two-way long-distance conversation took place on October 9, 1876, between Cambridgeport, Massachusetts, and Boston. Then, in 1915, AGB spoke on the first transcontinental telephone call. He was in New York, and far away in San Francisco was his assistant, Watson.

"Watson, come here. I want you!" said AGB, laughing.

"I'd be glad to come, Mr. Bell," replied Watson, "But it would take a week to come to New York from here!"

WILL SOMEBODY ANSWER THAT THING?!

What did AGB think of the telephone? When he worked in his lab, he often stuffed a towel around the phone so it couldn't interrupt him. "Now a man can think!" he would exclaim.

Make an old-fashioned phone call

How good were the first telephones? You can get an idea by trying this experiment. Get a group of friends in a circle and whisper a sentence or two to the friend next to you. That friend whispers the message to the friend next to her, and so on until it comes all the way back to you. Say it out loud, then tell your friends your original message. Do they sound alike? Let everyone take a turn making up a message.

Did you end up with a garbled, funny-sounding message every time? The first telephones often turned conversations into gobbledygook, too. Storms and even animals could cut off calls or make wires cross, so you might suddenly find yourself talking to a total stranger!

BELL NOISE

Next time you're blasting a CD and your dad shouts, "Turn that down a few decibels!!" ask him if he knows where "decibel" comes from. Like many words that begin with "dec," such as decade, it has to do with the number ten. A decibel is one-tenth of a bel and a bel is a measurement of sound. The bel was named for Alexander Graham Bell. Impressed? Hope your dad is too: he may not notice you didn't turn down the music!

23

The man behind the telephone: Alexander Graham Bell

When you think of AGB you probably think of the telephone, but AGB always thought he would be remembered for his many *other* inventions.

HD-4

Skimming the surface

High-speed boats now called hydrofoils that just skimmed the surface were another interest. In 1919 AGB's experimenters developed the fastest boat of its time: the *HD-4* skimmed along at 115 km/h (71 mph).

Silver Dart

Flying high

AGB was hooked on kites and flying. After many years of experimenting, his kite, the *Cygnet*, carried a man aloft for seven minutes on November 16, 1907. Then AGB moved on to planes. With the help of his Aerial Experiment Association, he created the *Silver Dart*, the plane that on August 27, 1909, became the first powered, heavier-than-air machine to fly in Canada. You can see a replica of it at the National Aviation Museum in Ottawa.

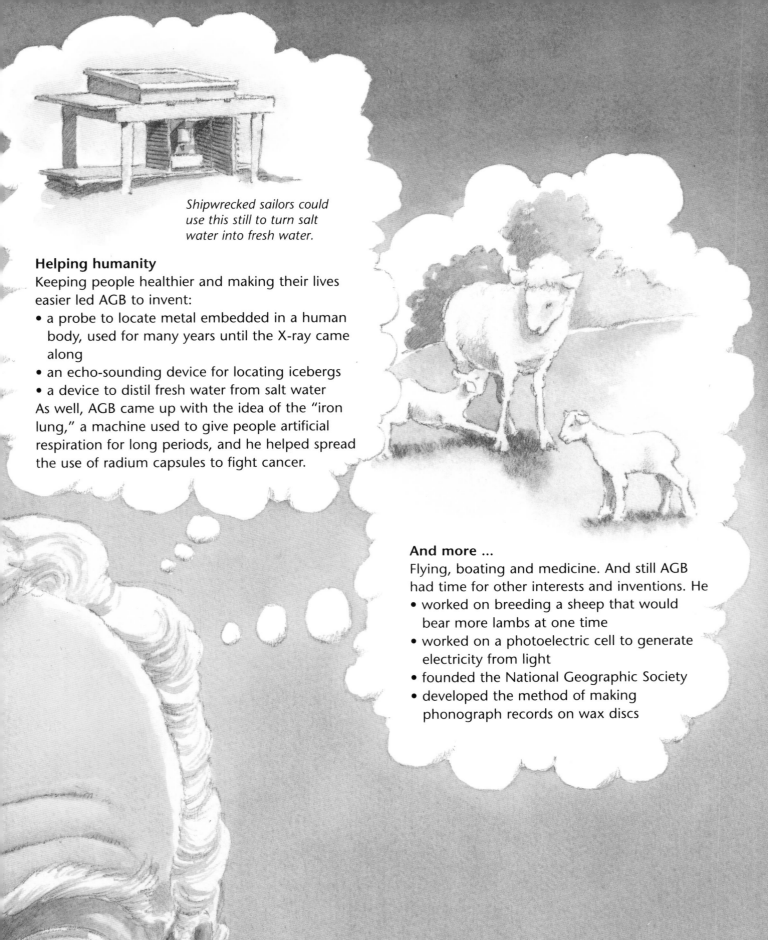

Shipwrecked sailors could use this still to turn salt water into fresh water.

Helping humanity

Keeping people healthier and making their lives easier led AGB to invent:
- a probe to locate metal embedded in a human body, used for many years until the X-ray came along
- an echo-sounding device for locating icebergs
- a device to distil fresh water from salt water

As well, AGB came up with the idea of the "iron lung," a machine used to give people artificial respiration for long periods, and he helped spread the use of radium capsules to fight cancer.

And more ...

Flying, boating and medicine. And still AGB had time for other interests and inventions. He
- worked on breeding a sheep that would bear more lambs at one time
- worked on a photoelectric cell to generate electricity from light
- founded the National Geographic Society
- developed the method of making phonograph records on wax discs

📷 *A phone family album* 📷

Meet some of the grandchildren and great-grandchildren of the first telephone on which Bell transmitted sound, called a gallows frame telephone. It got its name because it looked like a mini version of a gallows, the structure where criminals were hanged.

The phones you see here look old-fashioned now, but when they were created they were "high-tech" wonders. Which of these phones came first and which came last? Try to put them all in the correct order, then check your answers on page 63.

A. This phone is powered by a magneto, the same electric generator that puts the spark in the spark-plugs of many lawnmowers today. This was one of the first phones that could sit on your desk.

B. Telephone repairmen were used to having a receiver and a transmitter on the same handset. This phone made it available to ordinary people.

DROP IN ON DR. ALEXANDER GRAHAM BELL

AGB died at Baddeck, Nova Scotia, on August 2, 1922. The day he was buried, all railways and telephones in North America stopped for one minute.

You're a little too late to meet AGB himself, but you can still visit his homes and workshops. At the Bell Museum in Baddeck you'll see exhibits about him, as well as models of his inventions, including parts of the wooden hull of the *HD-4*. You can also drop in on AGB's home in Brantford, Ontario, or visit the Bell Room in the Smithsonian Institute in Washington, DC.

The Bell Homestead in Brantford

C. Here's an incredible idea — colour! Up until this time phones had been black. Hmmm. Did conversations get more colourful, too?

D. No, it's not a camera. It's the first telephone available in Canada.

E. You'd look this way too if you had a bell in your base. This was the first model that featured this innovation.

F. Notice the new feature — a separate receiver. When you turned the crank, you generated the power to call the operator.

G. The first telephone subscribers were probably tired and confused by the end of their conversations. A user had to switch the handset from mouth to ear to exchange news.

MAPLE LEAF OR BALD EAGLE?

AGB was often asked if the telephone was an American or a Canadian invention. Tough question! Although AGB had become an American citizen, he still loved Canada. He always explained diplomatically that he and Watson had made the telephone *work* in Boston on March 10, 1876, but that he had come up with the *idea* for the telephone almost two years earlier in Brantford, Ontario.

R-R-R-I-N-G!

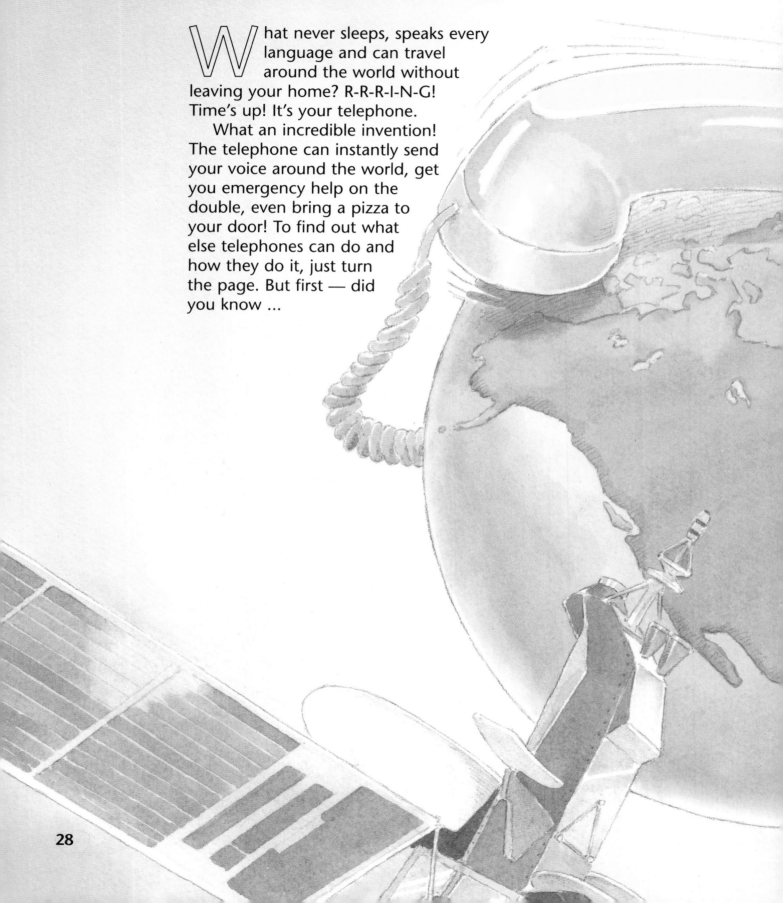

What never sleeps, speaks every language and can travel around the world without leaving your home? R-R-R-I-N-G! Time's up! It's your telephone.

What an incredible invention! The telephone can instantly send your voice around the world, get you emergency help on the double, even bring a pizza to your door! To find out what else telephones can do and how they do it, just turn the page. But first — did you know ...

There are more than 525 000 000 telephones in the world and they carry a total of 400 billion conversations each year.

The United States has more phones than any other country: 120 000 000.

Tokyo, Japan, has more than 5 511 000 telephones, making it the city with the most telephones in the world.

Between 10 and 11 A.M. on Mother's Day is the busiest hour for telephone calls on the busiest day of the year.

The smallest telephone in the world would fit comfortably in the palm of your hand.

The largest working telephone was 2.5 m (8 feet) high, 6 m (19 feet) long and weighed 3.5 tonnes (tons). The receiver was so heavy that it had to be lifted by a crane.

Who makes the most international phone calls? Americans are the winners, with their 5.4 billion minutes each year. Some other big talkers are:
Germans (2.47 billion minutes)
British (1.72 billion minutes)
French (1.57 billion minutes)
Swiss (1.01 billion minutes)

Canadians make over 33 billion local phone calls each year on 16 million telephones.

Inside your phone: at your end...

You've just seen the movie *Return of the Killer Bellybutton Lint* and you're dying to tell a friend about it. You pick up the phone and dial. Your "hello" starts up a complex chain of events that all take place in the blink of an eye.

The mouthpiece you speak into is like a miniature version of the microphones that rock stars use. It changes your voice into electric energy so it can be transmitted. How?

Hellllloooooo!

1. You speak into the microphone.

2. Your voice's sound waves hit a flexible **capacitor plate**. The vibrations of your voice put pressure on the plate and change its shape a little.

3. Each tiny change to the shape of the plate makes an electric signal vary, and those variations are carried out of your phone and along the **phone lines** as electric signals. To see what happens at the other end of the line, turn to page 32.

Your voice is changed into electric energy called an analogue signal. Analogue comes from the word "analogous," which means similar. But these analogue (A) signals are easily distorted by other signals. To make your conversations clear, the A signals are transmitted as digital (D) signals.

D signals are created by measuring the electric energy of your voice thousands of times a second. The energy is changed into just two types of pulses. That may not sound like much to transmit all the sounds your voice makes as you speak, but because your voice is measured or sampled so frequently, your phone transmits a very accurate version of it.

ANOTHER WAY TO GET THE WORD OUT

Older phones transmit sound using tiny particles of carbon instead of a capacitor plate. How can you tell what kind of phone you have? If your phone is built so that the mouthpiece unscrews, take it apart. **Ask permission first.** Give the little round mouthpiece a shake. Hear anything? A rattle-like sound means your phone uses particles of carbon rather than a capacitor plate.

(Carbon is used instead of, say, salt or pepper because it conducts electricity.)

Speak into a carbon granule mouthpiece and your voice makes a thin metal diaphragm vibrate. Those vibrations jostle the carbon granules and, as the granules move, they make an electric current vary. Just as in the microphones made with capacitor plates (they're called electret microphones), those variations are carried from your phone as electric signals.

... at your friend's end

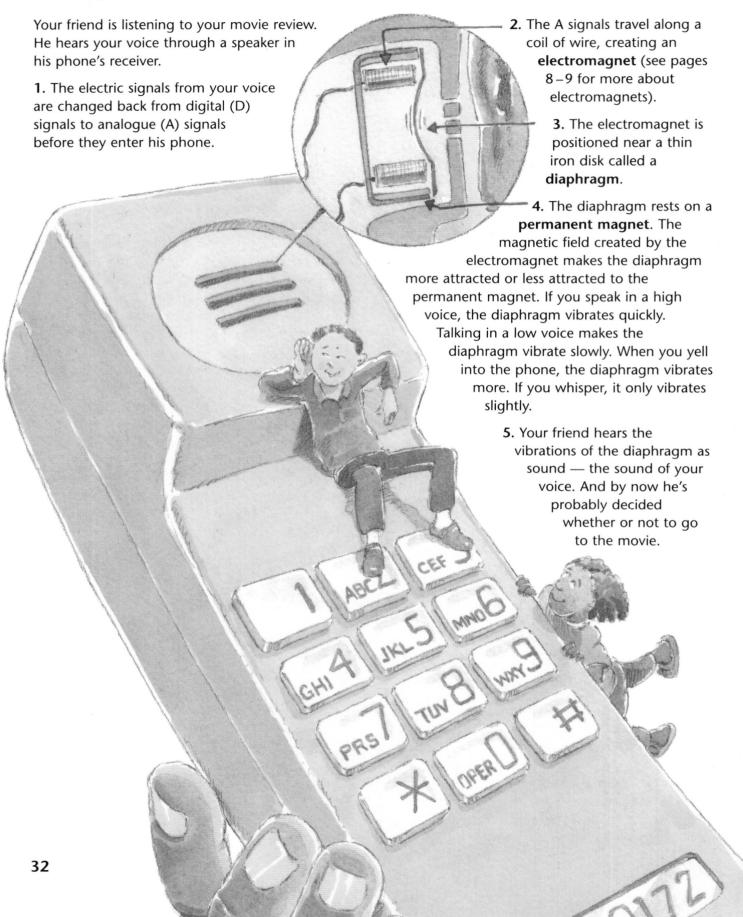

Your friend is listening to your movie review. He hears your voice through a speaker in his phone's receiver.

1. The electric signals from your voice are changed back from digital (D) signals to analogue (A) signals before they enter his phone.

2. The A signals travel along a coil of wire, creating an **electromagnet** (see pages 8–9 for more about electromagnets).

3. The electromagnet is positioned near a thin iron disk called a **diaphragm**.

4. The diaphragm rests on a **permanent magnet**. The magnetic field created by the electromagnet makes the diaphragm more attracted or less attracted to the permanent magnet. If you speak in a high voice, the diaphragm vibrates quickly. Talking in a low voice makes the diaphragm vibrate slowly. When you yell into the phone, the diaphragm vibrates more. If you whisper, it only vibrates slightly.

5. Your friend hears the vibrations of the diaphragm as sound — the sound of your voice. And by now he's probably decided whether or not to go to the movie.

(((((((*Good vibrations*)))))))

Hard to believe that your voice can affect capacitors or make particles move in a mouthpiece? Find out about sound energy with this experiment.

You'll need:
- a funnel
- a balloon
- a handful of rice cereal

1. Insert the funnel into the neck of the balloon and pour the rice cereal into it.

2. Blow up the balloon and tie the end closed.

3. Hold the balloon so that the cereal inside is close to your mouth. Try speaking loudly, softly, with a low voice and with a high voice. Watch what the cereal does.

What happens?
Sounds that carry a lot of energy, such as high-pitched sounds or loud sounds, make the cereal dance and vibrate. They transfer the energy to the cereal and the cereal reacts by moving. The carbon granules in the mouthpiece of your phone react the same way, depending on whether you whisper or yell into the phone. Electret microphones also react differently depending on what kind of energy is affecting them.
- Try repeating the experiment using smaller particles (such as crushed cereal, salt or pepper). Do smaller particles move differently?
- Try the experiment with a thicker or thinner balloon. What do you see?

EARMUFFS

Remember when you were telling your friend about that part in the movie when the bellybutton lint suddenly came pouring into the hero's bathroom? Your friend screamed, but his scream didn't sound very loud over the phone. That's because phones are carefully designed to turn down the volume on loud sounds that could hurt your ears. Inside the speaker a small device called a varistor limits the intensity of the electric signal that the speaker can transmit. Even when you scared your friend so badly that he dropped the phone, the crash wasn't as loud as it could have been — the varistor was at work protecting your ears.

Your phone's family

Your phone has a big family — all the phones that you and *your* family "talk" to. How does your phone stay in touch with all its relatives?

Your phone is connected to the rest of the phone system by wires that are often called lines. In some places you can see the lines overhead; in others, the lines are buried to protect them from storms, traffic accidents and other mishaps.

The lines from your house and your neighbours' homes all lead to a distribution plant, also called an outside plant. You've probably seen these plants many times but never really noticed them: they're grey-green metal boxes about the size of mailboxes with your phone company's logo on them, and they're located at the edge of lawns or at street corners. If you live in a large apartment building, your building probably has its own distribution plant in the basement.

34

A cable (a bundle of wires as thick as your wrist) leads from each distribution plant to a central office (CO). What does a CO look like? You may even have one right on your street and not know it. A CO may be disguised to look like a house or a small office building — again, look for the logo of your phone company.

The lines between your home and your CO are known as a local loop. If you call your next-door neighbour, or anyone else close by, your call goes through your CO. Each CO looks after an area of about 3100 hectares (12 square miles).

Suppose you want to call a friend who lives outside your neighbourhood? Your call is passed up the system. Each CO is connected to a toll office, which is connected to a primary office, which is connected to a secondary office, which is connected to a regional office. Whew! Your call gets up to the regional office level only if you're phoning across the country or around the world.

There are about 25 000 COs in North America, 1300 toll offices, 230 primary offices and 67 secondary offices. As well, North America has 12 regional offices, 10 in the United States and 2 in Canada (located in Regina and Montreal). At each level of the system, the lines can handle more and more calls. A device called a multiplexer lets one line carry several phone calls at the same time.

Answer the phone!

When a friend dials your number, your CO checks your line. If your phone is free, the CO sends out a ring signal, which flows along your line and makes a bell in your phone ring.

As you pick up your phone receiver, the two lines that bring the signal into your house touch and complete an electric circuit. (The same thing also happens whether you're answering the phone or picking it up to make a call.) An electric current flows between your phone and your CO. Now your phone is ready to receive the call.

If your phone is busy, your CO sends a signal to your friend's CO, and then her CO sends *her* a busy signal. A faster-than-usual busy signal means all the lines between you and your friend are busy. You probably hear this signal more often when you're making long-distance calls.

Got that long-distance feeling?

Belgium, India, Australia — it doesn't matter where your friends are scattered, your phone can still put you in touch with them instantly. In the process, your voice may be changed into light rays, bounced out to space or zapped along with the same technology that cooks your dinner.

ET, call home! ➤
Communication satellites are the cheapest way to send phone signals over extremely long distances.

About 36 000 km (22 320 miles) above the Earth, most of these satellites zoom along at approximately 30 000 km/h (18 600 miles per hour). They orbit Earth about as quickly as Earth rotates, so if you see one of these satellites, it never seems to move. (It has a geostationary orbit — "geo" means Earth.)

To transmit a call by satellite, the electric signals of your voice are changed into radio waves, beamed up to a communication satellite, then beamed back to Earth. Congratulations — you and your friend are now "uplinked." Each satellite can carry more than 1200 telephone voice signals in either direction.

▼ Have a light conversation
Optical fibres are sometimes used instead of wires to transmit telephone conversations. These fibres are thin strands of glass coated in plastic, each about as thick as a toothbrush bristle. There are anywhere from 12 to 200 optical fibres in a cable, and the larger cables can carry 40 000 calls at once.

Before your call can be carried by fibre optics, the sound energy of your voice must first be converted into electric signals and then into light signals. To do this, electric signals are fed into an encoder, then into a laser. The electric signals switch the laser on and off according to a code, and these encoded light signals are channelled into the optical fibre.

Light bounces off the sides of the glass fibre and speeds down the strand. At the other end, a photodetector picks up the signals and changes them back into electric signals — crystal clear in just microseconds.

DO YOU HEAR AN ECHO, ECHO, ECHO ...

Do you ever hear an echo when you're talking long distance? What you're actually hearing is your voice leaking. Huh? How can a voice leak? Instead of transmitting all of your voice to the person you're talking to (close by or long distance), phones are designed to let a little leak back to you, to make your voice sound better. This effect is called side-tone. Try speaking into a phone when it's unplugged. Hear the difference?

Your voice also leaks back to you from the phone of the person you're calling. So when you speak, you're actually hearing your voice from your end *and* your friend's end. That's okay when you and your friend are on nearby phones. However, on a long-distance call, the voice leaking from your friend's phone takes longer to get to your ear than the voice leaking from your own phone. So you hear your voice twice — like an echo.

To cut down on the echo, some satellite lines are equipped with an echo-cancelling device. When you talk, this shuts out sound leaking from your friend's phone. Sounds great — until your friend tries to interrupt you. You can't hear her, so you just keep talking. Bad communication.

▼ *Nuke a call*
In remote areas, microwaves may be used to send phone calls. The electric energy of your voice is converted into microwave signals. Those signals are relayed from tower to tower until they reach the one closest to your friend.
You know your call is being microwaved if you occasionally hear a beep as you're talking. The beep means the weather is interrupting the microwaves.

Take a number

Having a phone number is like having an address in the phone system. Your phone's address is a seven-digit number with a three-digit area code. What do the numbers mean?

The "1" signals your telephone company's central office (CO) that the caller wants to make a long-distance call, and the CO sends the call on to a toll office. A "0" would signal that the caller wants to make a long-distance call, but needs an operator's help in placing it.

These three numbers indicate the exchange in which the telephone is located. Each exchange in a city covers about 3100 hectares (12 square miles) and can accommodate 10 000 numbers, although only about 4100 are given out at any time. A central office (CO) takes care of one or more exchanges. There's usually some overlap so that if a CO is hit by a fire or some other disaster, all the phones in the neighbourhood won't be cut off. No exchange begins with "1" or "0," since these are both signals that the caller wants to make a long-distance call. To further avoid confusing local and long-distance calls, in many places in North America the second digit in a phone number won't be "0" or "1."

The next three numbers are the area code. Look at the area codes in the front of your phone book. Until recently the second digit was always a "0" or a "1" and the last digit was any number but "0." These are all signals that tell the CO the caller is dialling an area code. Now there are so many phones that area codes are being created that bend the rules.

The last four numbers identify the specific local loop in the exchange.

PHONE A JOKE

What's one of the most read books in your home? Probably the phone book. And once you get to know your phone book, you can use it to get a lot more than phone numbers.

First you need a touch-tone phone. (The signals from a rotary phone go only as far as the CO. The tones from a touch-tone phone can go past the CO to other systems. Also, sometimes you'll want to use the # and * signals. These signals don't exist on a rotary phone.) Now grab the phone book. Check out the front section of the Yellow Pages. In many places you can dial a daily horoscope, sports results, jokes, info on the latest hot songs or movies, updates on your favourite soap opera, recipes and lots more. Just make sure that the calls are free before you dial — if you're not sure, ask an adult, preferably one who pays the bills.

In France, phone books are already collector's items — they've been replaced by computers. If you move and change phone numbers, your listing can be instantly corrected or updated.

Hello, operator!

Is it 4-5 or 5-4? Why is it that you can never remember the last two digits in Ceri's phone number? Oh well, there's sure to be a phone book in that booth up ahead, so you can look up her number — again — and call her. But when you get to the phone booth, there's no book. Now what? Lucky for you, a telephone operator is just a call away.

Until the late 1880s you had to get an operator's help to place all telephone calls, even one to your next-door neighbour. You picked up the receiver and waited until an operator was free to help you. She (back then most operators were women) sat at a switchboard like the one you see here. She asked you whom you wanted to speak to, then put the plug of your phone line into the socket of your friend's phone, and the plug of your friend's phone line into the socket of your phone. Your friend's phone would ring and soon you'd be talking.

As more people installed telephones, switchboard rooms became bigger and bigger. Some held so many operators that the managers had to wear roller skates to get around the room quickly.

Not everyone thought this was a great system. Almon Strowger, an undertaker in Kansas City, was convinced that the telephone operators were sending potential customers to his rivals. And when Strowger placed calls himself, he would often get busy signals or wrong numbers. He was so upset that, in 1889, he designed what he called a "girlless, cussless telephone" — an automatic switching machine. For the first time callers could dial for themselves and the number was connected automatically.

And operators were still needed for long-distance calls. Back then, an operator would fill out a card called a toll ticket when you wanted to make a long-distance call. When the person you were calling answered his phone, the operator stamped the starting time on the toll ticket. At the end of the call, the operator stamped the time again and worked out the length and cost of the call. Whew! In order for long-distance calls to be on the automatic switching system, phone numbers across the country had to be standardized. The seven-digit phone number with a three-digit area code was born.

Today, operators are still available to help you find a phone number or make a long-distance call. Marine operators receive emergency calls and pass on coastguard information to ships. High-seas operators relay calls from ships far out at sea. Back on land, special emergency operators keep communications open during fires, accidents or other disasters.

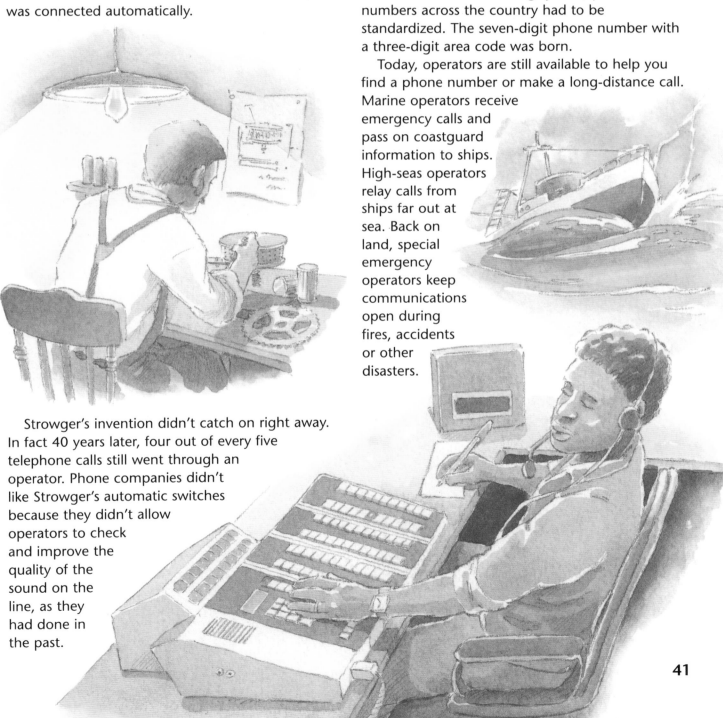

Strowger's invention didn't catch on right away. In fact 40 years later, four out of every five telephone calls still went through an operator. Phone companies didn't like Strowger's automatic switches because they didn't allow operators to check and improve the quality of the sound on the line, as they had done in the past.

Join a symphone-y orchestra

A touch-tone phone uses sound (called a tone) to dial a number. Equipment at your telephone company's central office hears the tones, identifies each number pushed, converts the information into a form it can transmit and dials the complete number.

When you push a button on a touch-tone phone, what you hear is actually a two-tone beep. Pick up the receiver and press 1 and then 4. The beeps sound different, but listen again — one of the tones is the same. Hang up, then lift the receiver and press 1 and 9. Are any of the tones the same?

All the numbers in one column on your key pad have one tone in common, and all the numbers in one row share a tone as well. So, for example, the 2 key has one tone in common with 1 and 3, and has a different tone in common with 5 and 8. Try it for yourself and see.

Once you know this secret, you can learn to play your phone and amaze your friends with your incredible musical talent. Be sure to try these terrific touch-tone tunes ONLY WHEN YOU'RE ALREADY TALKING TO SOMEONE. Otherwise you may be playing an expensive tune. And if you have a home security system, check with your parents to make sure it's not activated by the phone.

Happy Birthday to You

1 1 2 1 * 7
Hap-py Birth-day to you,
1 1 2 1 0 8
Hap-py Birth-day to you,
1 1 # *
Hap-py Birth-day,
0 0 9 8
Hap-py Birth-day
0 * # 0
Hap-py Birth-day to you.

Can you figure out what song this is?
6 5 4 5 6 6 6
5 5 5 6 # #
6 5 4 5 6 6 6
6 5 5 6 5 4
(Answer on page 63.)

"Hi, I'm not home right now ..."

How many times have you heard that message? An answering machine is like having your own private telephone operator. It listens to your phone line for calls. When the phone rings, the answering machine sends a signal saying the phone has been picked up (even though it really hasn't been), then it transmits its message and records the incoming message.

What sort of message do you think you might hear if you called someone famous? Try to match the answering machine messages to their owners, listed below. (Answers on page 63.)

a) Cleopatra
b) Lassie
c) Superman
d) Captain Picard
e) Elmer Fudd

1. Woof! Woof-woof! Woof! Woof-woof-woof!

2. I cannot answer your call right now because I'm on a mission. Engage.

3. I'm out hunting dat wascally wabbit.

4. Sorry, I'm not home. I'm having tea with King Tut and his mummy.

5. I can't answer the phone right now because I'm stuck in a phone booth.

PHONES AWAY FROM PHONE

Your phone number may be your address in the phone system, but what about when you're not at home. Pay phones are your phone away from home. There are even pay phones in the Antarctic! Know any penguins who might call you?

Phone on the run: cellular phones

Not again! You were supposed to pick up the vegetables for dinner tonight but you forgot. You can't ask your mom to pick them up because she's already on her way home. Wait a minute! She's just had a cellular phone installed in her car. As you dial her number you wonder if she'll mind making an extra stop — just this once.

How does your call get to her cellular car phone? First it goes to her cellular phone company's main office. Hundreds of telephone lines come in and end there. Then your call is converted to radio waves and beamed out to an antenna close to where your mom is driving.

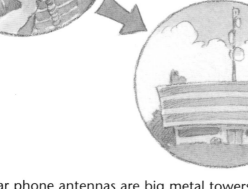

Cellular phone antennas are big metal towers about eight storeys high usually with round dishes near the top. You can see them in cities or on the edge of major highways. Each antenna serves a certain area called a "cell" — that's how cellular phones got their name.

The antenna nearest your mom sends the call out to her car phone. How does it know where to find her? Your mom's phone has two phone numbers: a regular phone number and a unique serial number. A cellular phone needs that serial number because it may be moving through an area in which another phone has the same seven-digit number. The serial number has to be unique in all of North America, so it's very long.

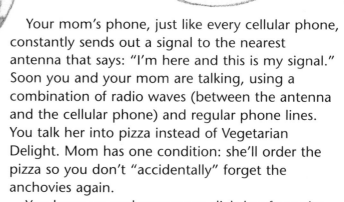

Your mom's phone, just like every cellular phone, constantly sends out a signal to the nearest antenna that says: "I'm here and this is my signal." Soon you and your mom are talking, using a combination of radio waves (between the antenna and the cellular phone) and regular phone lines. You talk her into pizza instead of Vegetarian Delight. Mom has one condition: she'll order the pizza so you don't "accidentally" forget the anchovies again.

You hang up and your mom dials her favourite pizza place. When she dials the number, a radio signal goes out to the nearest cellular phone antenna. From there the number goes to the cellular phone company's computer. The computer then dials the number just as if the call came from a regular phone. Your mom places her pizza order using radio waves and regular phone lines.

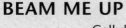

BEAM ME UP

Cellular phone "cousins" turn up all over the place. For instance, the individual satellite phones used by CNN reporters during the Gulf War are relatives. When a reporter sent news to North America, her cellular phone didn't "talk" to a local cell antenna — it talked to its own satellite dish. To transmit the call, the dish was pointed up at an orbiting satellite that would then pass the call overseas.

By the time your mom pulls into the driveway, your pizza has arrived. But, yippee! No anchovies! Your mom's about to phone and complain, but then she stops. As she gave the order, she was moving from one cell to another. For a split second, as the call was passed from one antenna to the next, it was interrupted. The word "anchovies" got lost in space.

As you dig into the pizza you wonder if you can arrange for your mom to order all your family's pizzas by cellular phone.

Emergency! Emergency!

You're walking home from school when you turn a corner and come across an accident. "Call an ambulance," someone yells. "No — the police," says another. Yet another voice orders you to phone the fire department. What do you do? Who should you call?

In most communities, you don't have to make a decision. Just dial 9-1-1 and an operator will send the help you need — fast.

Why a special three-digit number? People have a better chance of remembering a short number in a crisis. And they'll get the help they need faster, even if they're too weak to dial a regular seven-digit telephone number.

All 9-1-1 calls are carried over phone lines that handle only emergency calls. These lines have some amazing special features. If a 9-1-1 caller is too ill to speak, the operator can instantly trace the call and immediately send help. Using "call disconnect," the 9-1-1 operator can free a line even if the caller is too weak or sick to hang up. The "ringback" feature allows the operator to reconnect with a caller who may have accidentally disconnected. And "line freezing" lets the operator keep the line to the caller open for as long as necessary. The operator can stay with the caller and reassure her until help arrives.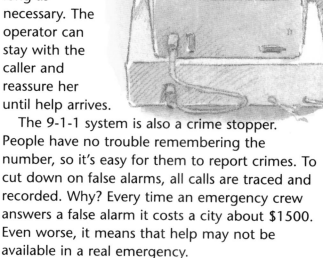

The 9-1-1 system is also a crime stopper. People have no trouble remembering the number, so it's easy for them to report crimes. To cut down on false alarms, all calls are traced and recorded. Why? Every time an emergency crew answers a false alarm it costs a city about $1500. Even worse, it means that help may not be available in a real emergency.

The system isn't perfect. Operators tell the story of a 9-1-1 call that came in with no one at the other end of the line, nothing but the barking of a dog. Was the caller too weak to speak or was someone preventing him or her from talking? The operator quickly traced the call and sent the police.

When the police arrived, no one answered the door. Fearing the worst, they forced their way into the house. Imagine their surprise when they found no victim, no crime, only a dog. It had knocked over the phone and stepped on a key programmed to call 9-1-1. Case closed.

If you have to call 9-1-1:
- Call only in a real emergency, when you need help *immediately*.
- Stay calm and speak slowly.
- Be ready to give your complete address.
- Don't stay on the line longer than you need to — other emergency calls need to get through.

NEED SOME HELP?

If you have a problem and no one to talk to, call the **Kids Help Phone**. Every day, more than 1200 kids call because they're depressed, having problems with their parents, pregnant, being abused or lots of other reasons. It doesn't cost anything and you can phone from anywhere in Canada. Call any time — there's always someone to help you. You don't have to give your name or tell your parents or friends about the call. No matter what your problem is, Kids Help Phone can help. Just call

1-800-668-6868

Special needs phones

Alexander Graham Bell was proud of the telephone not because it made him famous, but because it could help people. Phone inventors are still working to help make people's lives easier, especially people with disabilities who can't use regular telephones.

For people with hearing problems, there are phones with extra-loud ringers and volume controls on the receiver. (You can see a similar feature on some pay phones.) Other phones for the hearing impaired signal a call by flashing a light.

If you have a deaf friend you want to phone, it's no problem if he has an electronic teletypewriter connected to his telephone. You would dial his number, then type in your message on a machine that looks like a home computer. The message appears on your friend's "phone" screen. The letters TDD after a name in the phone book tell you the person uses this Telecommunication Device for the Deaf.

People who can't speak clearly can use special telephone receivers to amplify their voices. A person who is too weak to hold a receiver can put on a headset that weighs less than a dozen pennies. If she can't dial the phone, she can use the phone shown here. By blowing into the small plastic tube or touching a contact switch, she can receive or end calls. This special telephone can also connect a user with an operator who will help dial calls.

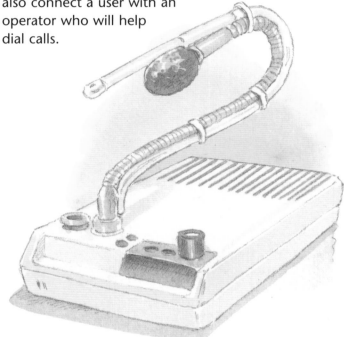

Push-button phones are the answer for people who are blind or are visually impaired. Phones with large numbers also make dialling easier for people with a loss of vision, and for those with a loss of motion, such as someone with cerebral palsy.

1-800-PAY-ZIPP

There's got to be a way to move up to the next level on the video game you got for your birthday. But how? You give up and call the 1-800 number on the package. Instantly you're in touch with the manufacturer across the country and the call doesn't cost you a cent.

You might say a 1-800 number is both an address and a stamp. When your central office receives an 800 number, it puts the call through and charges the call to that number. 1-800 numbers are also called WATS lines, which stands for Wide Area Telephone Service.

"HI, MAY I SPEAK TO THE FURNACE, PLEASE?"

Great! You're heading up to the family cottage for a ski weekend. The skis are on the roof-rack and the car is packed. Time to phone the cottage and turn on the heat. Phone the cottage? Yes, the same way you can access messages on an answering machine by pressing code numbers on

a touch-tone phone, you can turn on lights, start the hot-water heater bubbling and switch on other electric appliances with a phone call. All you need is a simple device that connects your cottage's appliances to the phone. "Oh, and by the way, cottage, please put the roast in the oven."

Fax facts

Looks like you've got another tricky-situation-of-the-month on your hands. You want to invite Malcolm to a surprise party for Kirsten, but you forgot to talk to him at school today. And you can't phone him up because Kirsten is studying at his place.

Suddenly you get a genius-type idea. You run to your mom's home office, press a few buttons and — zip! — without saying a word, Malcolm instantly has all the info. You faxed Malcolm the invitation. But hold the phone: you understand how phone lines transmit voices, but how do they send words — and even pictures?

Fax is short for facsimile (or exact copy). A fax machine sends a facsimile of a document or a photograph over the phone lines.

When you put your invitation into the fax, the machine seems to be "eating" the invitation, line by line. It's actually scanning the page in a series of thin lines. When the machine gets to the end of a line, it moves the paper along a bit and begins to scan again, right under the first line.

Light shines on the paper and is reflected off it onto photodetectors. White and light areas on the paper reflect more light than dark areas. The photodetectors transform this information into electric signals, which the fax machine sends over the phone line. The phone system passes along the fax signals as if they were a regular telephone call.

At the other end, Malcolm's fax machine decodes the signals into patterns of white and black, a line at a time, and prints them out.

Many fax machines use thermal paper, which has a special coating that turns dark when heated. (To see for yourself, hold a piece of fax paper near a warm light bulb. See the heated part turn colour?) Hundreds of tiny heaters in your friend's fax machine turn on and off to make the dark and light spots that form the letters on the page. Plain-paper faxes don't use heat to do their printing. Instead, a tiny laser printer does the job.

rollers

light source

photodetectors

Just the fax, ma'am

Fax from the past

You probably think the fax is a really modern invention, right? Would you believe it's older than the telephone?

Way back in 1842 Alexander Bain, a Scottish physicist and clock-maker, developed the electrochemical recording telegraph. (Catchy name, huh?) It transmitted pictures over a wire and onto special paper at the other end. Sounds a lot like a fax, doesn't it? However, Bain's machine used electrified pendulums. As a result, it was slow and expensive, so it never took off.

By 1907 there was already a fax system for sending photographs between London, Paris and Berlin. In 1922 a photo was transmitted from Rome to North America by radio and published in newspapers there on the same day. Newspapers depended on early fax machines to obtain photos of far-away places and events — fast.

The military has also used faxes for years. During the Second World War, photographs, maps, orders and weather charts sent by fax helped armies make battle plans.

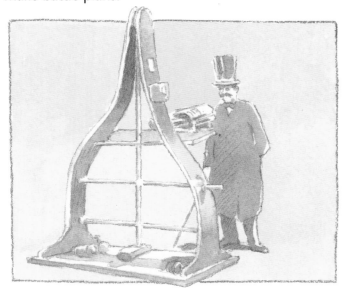

Here's how fax machines looked in the 1860s.

Fax to the rescue!

- Today, police fax photos, fingerprints and other evidence to police stations across the country or around the world to speed up identification of criminals.
- Firefighters use portable faxes to send reports and maps of the fire's progress to a centre coordinating emergency services.

- Doctors worried about a patient's heartbeat can fax a tracing to a far-away specialist, who can examine it and suggest treatment.

- Need lunch? Fax your order to your favourite fast-food restaurant.
- Staff in big offices sometimes fax a document to someone in the same office just to avoid the walk. Forget about couch potatoes — now there are "fax potatoes"!

Fax to the max

Got a l-o-o-ng letter you want to send to a friend? The largest fax machine can now transmit documents up to 90 cm (35 inches) wide and up to 60 m (197 feet) long.

Itty-bitty fax

The smallest fax machine is only a little larger and thicker than a deck of cards.

On your mark, get set, FAX!

Now it takes up to 40 seconds to fax a page, but soon it will take five seconds — and the fax will look a lot clearer, too.

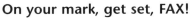

Return to sender?

Faxes from the other side of the world are common, but what about faxes from the other side of the grave? Workers at an insurance office in Britain were shocked to receive what seemed to be a fax from a co-worker who had died a few days earlier in a car accident. First came a picture of him, looking calm and serene, then a message describing life in heaven. What next? New song lyrics from Elvis?

FAX A GAME

Feel like a game of chess with your best friend across town? If you both have fax machines you can fax your moves back and forth.

What other games can you play by fax? How about Tic-tac-toe, Scrabble and Hangman. Or try Battleships — you won't have to worry about your friend spying on your board when you're playing by fax. One piece of advice: don't play games long distance or your fun could cost you more than just the game.

Party lines

Organizing Kirsten's surprise party is turning out to be a pain. Every time you tried to talk to your friends about it today at school, Kirsten appeared. Maybe it'll be easier to arrange by phone. Sure beats doing homework.

Luckily, you've programmed most of your friends' numbers into the Speed Dial feature on your phone. Andrew's first on your list, so you punch in his code. While you wait, your phone dials the number that you preprogrammed. Your telephone company's central office (CO) receives the same signal as if the complete number had been dialled and places your call. Success! Andrew can come to the party!

Jocelyn's next on your list and she's on Speed Dial, too. But — uh-oh — her line is busy. Your telephone to the rescue again! Punch in Call Again and take a break while your phone keeps trying her. Call Again sends a signal to your CO to watch Jocelyn's line and let you know when it's free. When she hangs up, her CO tells your CO, "She's finally done!" Your CO then sends a ring to your phone, a ring that sounds a little different from your regular one. When you pick up your receiver, your CO automatically calls Jocelyn's number as if you'd dialled it.

When you call Brett the voice answering his phone sounds like your friend Paul. "It *is* Paul," he says, "Brett forwarded his calls here." Call Forwarding let Brett tell his CO to send his calls to Paul's number. You tell Paul and Brett about the party and hang up.

Suddenly your phone rings. As you pick it up you glance at the Call Display. Your CO knows what number is calling and sends the info as a series of tones after the first ring.

The phone's display screen translates the tones into a phone number and — oh no, it's Kirsten! Call Screening would have helped you avoid her. When her call came in, your CO would have checked whether to connect it. If you'd programmed in a code telling it not to, Kirsten would have been shut out. You get off the phone as quickly as you can.

Next on your list is Alix. "Hi," she says, "Can I call you back? I'm talking to Sandy." Alix must have Call Waiting. When you called, her CO checked to see if her line was free. It wasn't. But the CO didn't give up. It sent Alix a beep to let her know she has a call waiting. Alix can ignore the beep or she can briefly hang up, or "flash," her phone. Then her CO puts Sandy on hold and connects you. Alix can get back to Sandy by "flashing" again. You tell Alix about the party and ask her to tell Sandy.

While you're talking to Jasmine, *your* Call Waiting beeps. But before you can get to it the call is gone. Your phone's equipped with Call Return so returning that call is no problem. By pushing a few buttons, your phone lets you know what number just called you and with a push of another button, your CO will connect you with it.

This whole process would have been a lot easier if you had a voice-activated phone. You could just say "Marilyn" and in seconds her line would ring. Your phone would analyse your voice and match it to a voice print you'd preprogrammed.

Whew! You finally made all your calls. Now, about that homework ...

TOMORROW TODAY

Ya-a-a-awn! What a great sleep! You feel as if you've slept for a hundred years. But now it's time to get up because you've got things to do before you switch on school. First, check your computer. Gretchen in Lisbon promised to send you that new Proton game, and Matt in Australia — or is it Belgium? — wanted some help with his modem. Oh, yeah — you promised to phone Graham with details for the party on Friday. You dial him on your wristwatch phone as you race down to breakfast and ...

Wait a minute — switch on school? Chatting on your computer with friends from around the world? Wristwatch phone? Maybe you *were* under a magic spell and *did* sleep for a hundred years.

Or maybe it's the magic of the telephone ...

Be my phone
Someday soon you'll be able to "personalize" almost any phone. How? Just insert your personalized phone card and program the telephone company's computer to reroute your calls, faxes and messages to the nearest phone.

"Help! I'm stuck in a fax booth!"
Some pay phones already have faxes built into them. Other pay phones can be transformed into computers. By inputting the correct code, you can tap into weather information, business reports, whatever!

"Tracey calling Tess"
Remember Dick Tracey's wristwatch phone? Now it's more than just a cartoon fantasy. With the push of a button on this lightweight phone you're immediately in touch with your friends.

That's two and 15 zeros
By the year 2000, experts estimate there will be 2.5 billion telephones in the world and they'll carry a total of 2 quadrillion — that's 2 000 000 000 000 000 — calls each year!

Pass me the *Telephone Weekly*, will ya?
Some researchers believe that in the future you'll receive TV signals over fibre-optic phone lines. This TV/phone service will be cheaper and the quality better than the television you watch today.

Networks of tomorrow: 1

On page 31 you read how your voice is converted from an analogue signal to a digital signal as you make a telephone call. But in the not-too-distant future, a new system will change that — and give your telephone some amazing capabilities.

The new system is called the Integrated Services Digital Network, or ISDN. With ISDN, your telephone, rather than your central office, will convert analogue signals (your voice) to digital signals. The result? Your telephone will look different from your current phone — and act differently, too.

Today's phones transmit dialling information (the number you're calling) and conversation (or fax) on one wire. But ISDN will use *two* networks to transmit a call. One network will carry the dialling information — it's called the data, or D, channel. The other network will carry the actual conversation (or fax) — it's called the bearer, or B, channel.

ISDN will allow you to make a call from your bedroom while your dad is on the same line in the kitchen. Doctors and hospitals will be able to transmit patients' entire medical history, including complicated X-rays, ultrasound images and CAT scans. And that's just the beginning.

Team up computers with ISDN and watch out! Step into the school of the future and see for yourself. You sit down at your computer to present your project on the importance of mountain bikes way back in the 1990s. You dial up your teacher and then each of your classmates. As you reach them, their pictures show up on your screen.

Nervously, you clear your throat and begin your presentation. It's going smoothly until your teacher stops to ask a question. Whew! That wasn't too tough, but you find it hard to get back on track. Maybe now would be a good time to show a video on biking. In seconds the video is playing on

everyone's computer screen and you can relax.

Uh-oh, break's over. You call up a bicycle engineer you met while doing your research. His picture appears at the top of your screen and soon he's answering questions from everyone in the class. Simon comes up with a tricky question, but the engineer isn't stumped. He calls up an expert of his own. To answer Simon's question, she produces a page of documentation and soon everyone in your class is reading it on their screens.

Suddenly your computer beeps. Time to connect with Moon Colony 5 and find out about mountain biking there. You watch some experiments and get a commentary from the scientist in charge.

Time's up! You thank the scientist and sum up your report. Your teacher compliments you on your good work. Then she hands out a math test. Now if only ISDN could help you with that!

You can already share information on your computer with a friend's computer — thanks to your telephone.

To transmit computer data, you first have to convert it into sounds. This process is called modulation and it's done by a modem. (Bet you wondered how it got its name.) You and your friend each connect your computers to modems and the modems are connected to the telephone line. When the modem receives sounds from another computer, it "demodulates" them into data.

Modems can also connect you to collections of information called databases. You can find out what books are available in libraries, play games with other users, or connect with a "bulletin board" that tells you who to contact if you need help with your computer, want to discuss last night's football game and many other things.

Bulletin boards are great for local information, but if you want information from around the world, take a ride on the information highway. Phone lines provide the roadway for the information to move along. You can connect with anyone on the system — called the Internet — and get information or E-mail (electronic mail) back. It's a great way to gather statistics on another country for your geography essay or discover some really wild computer games!

Networks of tomorrow: 2

"Congratulations," the doctor says. "You have a healthy new baby."

"Thank you, doctor," you say, then go back to cooing and whispering at the sweet little red and wrinkly face.

"Congratulations," says a representative of the phone company. "I'd like to present your baby's very own PCN."

PCN?? What have you just done to your child? PCN stands for Personal Communication Network or Number. By the time you're old enough to be a parent, your child might be assigned a PCN at birth that he will use for the rest of his life. A PCN is a person's unique telephone number. You might

live in a homeful of people, but you'd each have your own PCN. To reach you, friends would dial your special number.

Today we call places and hope the person we want is there. With PCN, you'd call people. So, for instance, if you had several part-time jobs, friends wouldn't have to track you down by phoning many places — they'd just dial your PCN and find you wherever you were.

Would this mean carrying around your own personal phone? Probably — you'll likely have your own cordless phone, small enough to fit in your pocket. People are already using cordless phones to transmit or receive calls within 180 m (590 feet)

TALK ON THE RUN

Welcome back to the 1990s! Gus the wonder cat has decided that your science project is a lot more fun than his catnip mouse and he's running off with it to his favourite hiding place behind the sofa. You're tearing down the hall after Gus when the phone rings. It's your mom with some dinner instructions. How are you going to retrieve your project *and* find out how to prepare Tofu Surprise at the same time? No problem if you have a cordless phone. You can run and talk at the same time. A cordless phone uses radio waves to transmit the dial and voice info. It has a base that stays put and is connected to your phone line and usually to an electric outlet, too. The handset is the part you can take with you anywhere around your home or back yard. It's powered by a battery that you recharge at the base.

But beware — if your cordless is on the same channel as your neighbours', your phone may ring when *they* get a call. Or your calls may be interrupted by remote-control toys, TV remotes, even garage-door openers. To prevent interruptions, most cordless phones can be switched to one of nine other channels.

of a base station. With PCN, thousands of base stations would be installed on the walls of buildings or about a metre (3 feet) above the ground on posts. At home, you'd have your own base station, about the size of a textbook. Offices would have slightly larger versions to deal with many more calls.

PCN phones will be a lot cheaper and lighter than cellular phones — only 85 to 140 g (3 to 5 ounces). And already a feature called "roaming" allows you to use the PCN and a cellular phone or pager to contact someone anywhere in North America where there's a cellular-phone network.

Maybe PCN should stand for Pretty Cool Network.

What's next?

AGB would probably have a hard time recognizing his invention today. Bringing you information from around the world, getting your calls to you no matter where you are, transmitting sounds, words, pictures — who knows what else is in the future? If you could invent a new telephone, what would you most like it to do?

IT'S FOR YOUUU!

Beam me over to my friend's when I call her.

Answer the call, then page whoever is wanted.

Transport things I've ordered from the store.

Come when I call it and follow me around the house.

Do my homework!

GLOSSARY

analogue signals: signals that are similar to another set of signals, in that they vary in strength in the same way

database: a collection of information that can be accessed by computer

diaphragm: a thin sheet of skin, metal, etc. that can vibrate in response to a force, such as sound or an electromagnet

digital signals: signals created by measuring the electric energy of your voice thousands of times a second

eardrum: a thin membrane (skin) in the ear that vibrates in response to sound

electromagnet: coils of wire wrapped round an iron core that become a magnet when electricity passes through the coils

electronic mail (E-mail): a system that uses computers and telephone lines to send and receive messages

fax (facsimile) machine: a machine that scans documents or pictures and sends a copy over telephone lines

laser: a device for producing a narrow beam of very pure light

microwaves: radio waves of very high frequency that can be used to send telecommunication signals

modem: a device for converting computer data into sounds (and back again) for transmission over telephone lines

optical fibres: thin strands of glass that send signals in the form of pulses of laser light

satellite: a device that orbits Earth and can transmit telecommunication signals

telecommunication: communication, often over large distances, by telephone, telegraph, computer, etc.

telegraph: a device for transmitting messages or signals over wire by making and breaking electric connections

telephone: a device for transmitting sound, especially speech, by wire, radio, microwaves, etc., by converting sound vibrations to electric signals

---

ANSWERS

A phone family album, pages 26-27
1 D: 1877, 2 G: 1878, 3 F: 1879, 4 A: 1881, 5 B: 1927, 6 E: 1937, 7 C: 1955.

Join a symphone-y orchestra, page 42
The song is "Mary Had a Little Lamb."

"Hi, I'm not home right now ...", page 43
1b, 2d, 3e, 4a, 5c.

INDEX